For P.B.
And to the (very silly) bear on the hill in Yosemite Park
- *you know who you are!*

First published in hardback in 2001 by Egmont Books Limited
This edition published in 2006 by Egmont UK Limited
239 Kensington High Street, London W8 6SA
Text and illustrations copyright © Jan Fearnley 2001
Jan Fearnley has asserted her moral rights
A CIP catalogue record for this title is available from the British Library

Printed in Malaysia

ISBN 978 1 4052 2701 8

3 5 7 9 10 8 6 4 2

This book belongs to

# A Perfect Day For It

### Jan Fearnley

EGMONT

IT WAS A BEAUTIFUL,
crisp winter morning.
Bear stepped out into the snow
and sniffed all around him.
His merry little eyes twinkled
in the bright light.
His big, furry feet crunched the
fresh white snow under his toes.
He licked a claw and held it into
the chill morning breeze.

**"PERFECT!"** he said.
Bear had a plan. He smiled
and set off for the mountain.

"GOOD MORNING, BEAR," said Badger. "Where are you going?"
"Up the mountain, my little friend," Bear replied.
"What for?" asked Badger nosily.
"Because it's a perfect day for it," said Bear, and off he went tramp tramp tramp up the snowy mountain track.

"He's up to something," said Badger.
"I bet he's going to find some of his secret
**honeycomb!**"
Badger's mouth watered at the thought of
sweet, sticky honey oozing from the comb.
"Such a shame to let Bear struggle on his
own. I'd better go along to help him eat it."

So Badger went scritchity **scratchity** up
the hill, hurrying to catch Bear,

and Bear went
tramp **tramp** tramp
up the snowy mountain track.

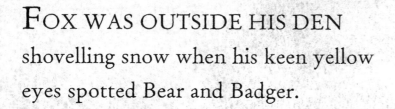

FOX WAS OUTSIDE HIS DEN shovelling snow when his keen yellow eyes spotted Bear and Badger.

"They're up to something!" he said to himself. "I bet they're planning to **snowball** someone! What fun! But they'll need a sharp eye and some cunning. I'd better go along too."

So Fox went
paddypaw **paddypaw**
over his frozen path,

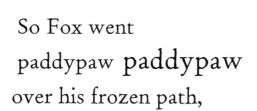

Badger went scritchity **scratchity**

and Bear went
tramp tramp tramp
up the snowy mountain track.

SQUIRREL WAS SITTING in the tree-tops, watching her friends climbing higher and higher up the mountain.

"They're up to something!" she said to herself. "I bet they're looking for buried **treasure!**" Squirrel thought about her own little treasure store of nuts buried at the foot of her tree. She felt very excited. "I'm an expert at finding treasure and they'll be hopeless. I'd better go along too, just to help."

So squirrel scampered
down her tree – tippytoes **tippytoes**
– picking her way in the snow,
following her friends,

*paddypaw* paddypaw

and tramp tramp tramp up the snowy mountain track.

scritchity scratchity

SQUIRREL WAS IN SUCH A HURRY, she nearly trod on Mole.

"They're up to something!" said Mole to himself. "I bet they're off to find some **bugs** and **worms**!"

Mole's tummy rumbled at the thought
of some juicy, slimy, wriggly worms.

"Yum yum, my favourite!" he said.
"I'd better go along too."  And he slid
down the icy path after his friends.
Slippy slidey bump!

paddypaw paddypaw

scritchity scratchity

and Bear went
tramp **tramp** **tramp**
up the snowy mountain track.

BEAR GOT A BIG SURPRISE when
he looked back over his shoulder and
discovered that he'd been followed.

He chuckled to himself and kept
on climbing.

UP, **UP**, **UP** he went, until
he had reached the summit.
Then he stopped.

"PERFECT!" he said to himself.

Bear sat down on his big furry bottom
and had a little rest.

BEAR LOOKED AT THE beautiful view – the trees, the valley – and the excited faces of his friends as they crowded all around him.

"Where's the **honeycomb**?" asked Badger.

"Honeycomb? What about the **snowballing**?" said Fox.

". . . Where are the juicy **bugs**?" butted in Mole.

"Bugs, what kind of **treasure** is that!" said Squirrel. "Yeuch!"

BEAR TWIDDLED HIS TOES
in the snow.

"I never said I was climbing up here for
**honeycomb**, or **snowballing**,
or **bugs**, or even **treasure**."

The animals were confused and cross.

"But you said it was a **perfect** day
for it," Badger grumbled.
"We've come all this way for nothing!
It's very cold up here, you know."

Bear threw back his big shaggy head and **laughed**, so loudly it echoed around the valley.

"What's so funny?" grumbled the others. "Some perfect day this is!"

"**But it is** a perfect day for it," chuckled Bear.

"Climb aboard, and I'll show you."

BEAR LAY ON HIS TUMMY
and his friends clambered onto his
big, broad back.

"Now," said Bear, "it really is a **perfect** day, a **wonderful** day, a truly **magnificent** day and the best reason I know for climbing up the mountain **is** . . .

...So YOU CAN SLIDE back down again!
Hold on tight!"